Praise for Baptism & Boomerangs

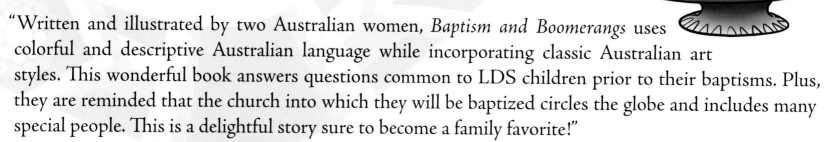

"Written and illustrated by two Australian women, *Baptism and Boomerangs* uses colorful and descriptive Australian language while incorporating classic Australian art styles. This wonderful book answers questions common to LDS children prior to their baptisms. Plus, they are reminded that the church into which they will be baptized circles the globe and includes many special people. This is a delightful story sure to become a family favorite!"

—Marilyn Bushman-Carlton, author of *Pulchritudinous* and *Other Ways to Say Beautiful*

"*Baptism and Boomerangs* is fresh, delightful, and profound. Written in clear, accessible language, this book puts a new 'spin' on understanding the power and purpose of baptism. With unique images, a broad cultural view, and lots of fun, this book will be one your children will come back to again and again."

—Linda Hoffman Kimball, author of *Apple Pies and Promises* and *Chocolate Chips and Charity*

"Sherrie Gavin's narrative weaves together powerful themes: the familiarity of home; the warm affection of earthly family; the hard, repetitive work of learning righteousness; and the hope of return to our heavenly parents. The location of this quintessentially Latter-day Saint story in Australia speaks to the unity of a covenant people within a global church."

—Melissa Inouye, associate editor of the *Mormon Studies Review*

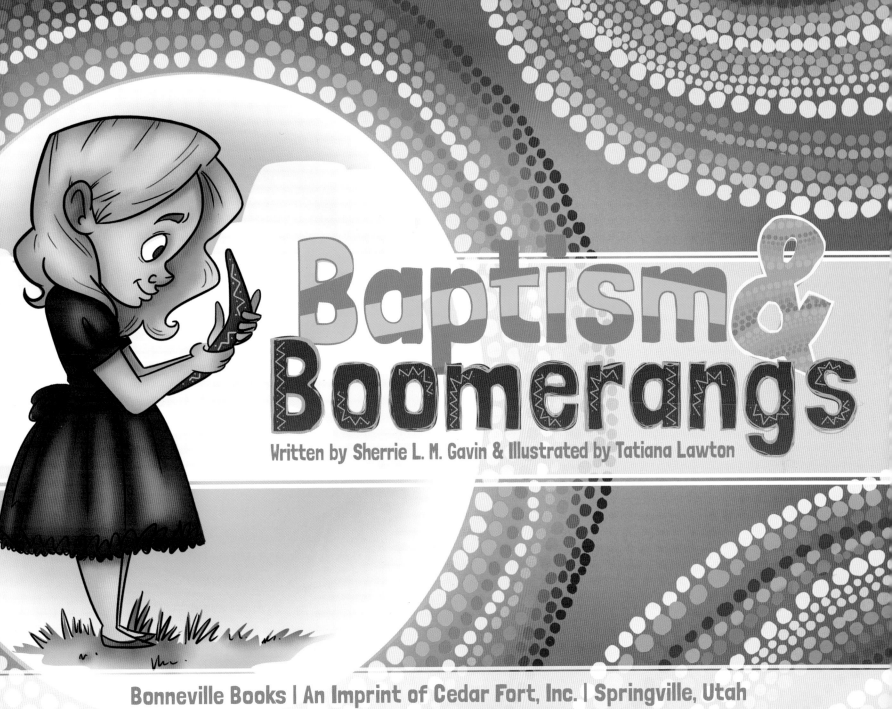

Baptism & Boomerangs

Written by Sherrie L. M. Gavin & Illustrated by Tatiana Lawton

Bonneville Books | An Imprint of Cedar Fort, Inc. | Springville, Utah

ISBN 13: 978-1-4621-1681-2

Published by Bonneville Books, an imprint of Cedar Fort, Inc.,
2373 W. 700 S., Springville, UT 84663
Distributed by Cedar Fort, Inc., www.cedarfort.com

LIBRARY OF CONGRESS CATALOGING-IN-PUBLICATION DATA

Gavin, Sherrie.
  Baptism and boomerangs / Sherrie Gavin.
     pages cm
  Summary: Amara wants to be with her grandparents when she is baptized, so soon after her eighth birthday she, her parents, and her brother, Jack, go to Sydney, Australia, where Grandad uses a lesson in throwing a boomerang to explain the sacrament of baptism and its effects.
  ISBN 978-1-4621-1681-2 (hard back : alk. paper)
  [1. Baptism--Fiction. 2. Boomerangs--Fiction. 3. Church of Jesus Christ of Latter-day Saints--Doctrines--Fiction. 4. Mormons--Fiction. 5. Family life--Australia--Fiction. 6. Australia--Fiction.] I. Title.
  PZ7.1.G38Bap 2015
  [Fic]--dc23
                        2014045822

Cover and page design and typography by Michelle May
Cover design © 2015 by Lyle Mortimer
Edited by Melissa J. Caldwell

Printed and bound in China

10 9 8 7 6 5 4 3 2 1

Printed on acid-free paper

"I think I see him!" Mum said outside the Sydney airport.

Moments later, an enormous vehicle pulled up.

"G'day!" called out Grandad. Amara leaped into his arms once he opened his door. "I've missed you the most," he said warmly. And with his very special Grandad smile, he added, "You and Jack, of course."

Amara thought about Grandad's smile as he began to drive; she didn't know how he did that with his smile, but it was something that only her Grandad could do. When he smiled, it was like he was laughing, playing a game, and comforting her all at the same time.

"Your Grandma and I sure are excited to see you," he said to Amara with his smile. Then with an extra twinkle in his eyes, he asked, "Are you still planning on getting baptized?"

"Yes!" Amara giggled. "That's why we came! Not just for my birthday."

Amara had looked forward to turning eight years old for as long as she could remember so that she could be baptized. Even though her real birthday was two weeks earlier, she wanted Grandma and Grandad to be at her baptism, so she decided to wait to have her special day with them.

When they got home, everyone gathered around Amara's birthday cake. It was a Jaffa cake, Amara's favorite! Amara thought about her baptism. This wasn't ordinary birthday cake—it was her eighth birthday cake. In a way it was baptism cake. She took a deep breath and blew out the candles.

"Oh no!" she said. "I forgot my birthday wish."

"You can save it for later," said Mum. Amara nodded and ate a slice. Swirls of orange and chocolate danced in her mouth.

Her heart felt a little nervous. It felt like frightened butterflies were jumping around, trying to tickle her. Did these nervous butterflies know something she didn't? She knew that being baptized would make her feel different. But Amara could not imagine exactly what kind of different it would feel like. The more she thought about it, the more she worried.

"What is on your mind, Amara?" Mum said softly.

Amara was quiet for a moment and saw all her family's eyes on her.

"Um . . ." She wasn't sure what to say. "It's just . . ." She took a deep breath. "What happens after? Why do we even get baptized?"

"We've talked about this," said Dad with an understanding smile. "We need to follow Jesus Christ. He was baptized, and we need to be baptized to belong to His church."

"You get the Holy Ghost after!" Jack shouted happily.

"Okay," Amara said. She was embarrassed to admit that she was still worried.

"Hey, maties," Grandad called to her and Jack the next morning.

"Grandma and your mum went to the shops and your dad is organizing the barbecue. So," he said, smiling his special smile while wriggling his eyebrows up and down, "we have the morning to ourselves! What shall we do?"

"Let's go to the park!" Amara said at the same time Jack yelled, "The park!"

Grandad smiled. "I thought we'd give these boomerangs a go."

"Wow!" said Jack. "Really?"

"Yep. Boomerangs are a must when there is a baptism."

"What?" said Amara. She stopped for a moment to think about baptisms and boomerangs. After a second, she regained her footing and hurried to catch up with Grandad, who was setting a bag on the grass. "Baptism goes with boomerangs? But how?"

"Well," said Grandad, "you asked a great question last night. What happens after baptism?"

"You put dry clothes on!" said Jack.

Grandad laughed. "Yes . . . and then?"

"You get confirmed," said Amara.

"And then?"

Amara and Jack were quiet. "I guess we don't know," Amara said, shrugging her shoulders.

Amara and Jack helped Grandad lay out the blanket, and Grandad pulled out the boomerangs. "Let's start with baptism. Now, there's no way to sugarcoat a crocodile."

"Is getting baptized dangerous?" asked Jack.

"No." Grandad laughed and flashed his perfect smile. "Not at all. Baptism isn't dangerous. It's exciting!" Grandad took one of the boomerangs. "See the curve of the boomerang. On this side, the edge is shaved down just a touch. This shape is what makes it come back when we throw it."

Amara and Jack inspected the boomerang. It was shaped like short arms stretched in a V. One arm looked perfectly rounded, smooth and flat. The other arm on the opposite side had a small shaved area in a section as long as Amara's thumb.

"Our Heavenly Parents created a perfect plan so we could return to them," Grandad said. "The boomerang's shape is like that perfect plan. It is perfectly shaped to return."

Amara ran her fingers around the boomerang, stopping at the shaved edge. "And that shaved edge?" Grandad said. "That is how the boomerang starts its journey. Just like baptism. Baptism is the start of our journey to return to live with our family and our Heavenly Parents forever."

Jack grabbed his boomerang and threw it. It fell flat on the ground.

"It didn't work," he said.

"Hang on there, Jack," said Grandad. "You need to throw it the right way. Just like we need to live our lives the right way. Then it will return. Let me show you."

Grandad took the boomerang by the side without the shaved edge and held it out like an upside down V, almost at arm's length in front of his shoulder. He cast the boomerang in the air with a sharp downward flicking motion, directly out to the open park area. The boomerang whirred, then rounded and headed back to Grandad. "Look out!" Amara squealed. She and Jack laughed as they watched Grandad catch the boomerang by slapping it between his hands.

"We want to try!"

Grandad handed each of them a boomerang. They tried throwing it the way Grandad had but without any luck. Each time they threw the boomerang, it fell to the ground.

"This is too hard!" Amara said, getting cranky. "I can't do it."

"Yes, you can," said Grandad, still smiling. "It can be hard at first, but you keep working at it. It's like taking the sacrament on Sundays. After you are baptized, when you take the sacrament, it is as if you have been baptized again. You start fresh. Learn from the mistakes. Then go again."

Amara looked at the boomerang and thought about how Grandad looked when he threw it—how he stood and how he moved.

Grandad spoke again. "If you throw the 'rang and it drops, pick it up, think about how to do better, and try again. Every time you try, you try your best."

"I thought I might find you here." Amara heard her mum's voice and looked up to her smiling face. Amara noticed that Mum's smile was very much like Grandad's.

"We're throwing boomerangs!" said Jack.

"And talking about baptism," said Amara.

"We can't get the boomerangs to come back yet," said Jack.

"But we're still trying," said Amara.

"You know," said Mum. "Grandad taught me about baptism and boomerangs when I was your age."

"He did?" asked Amara.

"Yes. But there is something else to remember," she said. "We are all here to help."

"Help with what?" said Amara.

"Your Dad and I are here to help you know right from wrong. Plus, you get the Holy Ghost who will guide who you to the right path. You still have to do the work. But you have a team to help you. When you are on the path to return to your Heavenly Parents, you are never alone."

Amara hugged her mother. "I love you, Mum."

"I love you too, Amara."

That afternoon, Amara was baptized. Amara felt peaceful and happy as her Dad performed the baptism. She was thrilled when Grandad gave a talk about baptism, and then presented her with a boomerang that had her name painted in her favorite color. Every word Mum said in her talk on the Holy Ghost felt like a warm hug meant especially for Amara.

While the grown-ups were talking, Amara went outside to try her boomerang in the large grassy area behind the church. She was not having any luck. She remembered that she still had a birthday wish from the candles on her cake. But a wish didn't feel right. She decided to say a silent prayer.

As she finished her prayer, she heard a soft voice behind her. "Are you still throwing your 'rang?" Jack asked.

"Yes."

"Any luck getting it to come back?"

"No."

"Can I help?"

Suddenly, Amara felt something good inside her heart. She was happy that Jack wanted to help her. "Yes!" she said. "Please!"

She and Jack worked on throwing the boomerang properly, each taking turns and trying to help each other. When the boomerang finally came back, they weren't sure who had thrown it. She and Jack were so excited that they jumped and laughed and didn't notice Grandad watching.

"Good on ya!" he shouted. "I knew you could do it!"

"Thank you, Grandad!" said Amara, excitedly skipping and jumping toward Grandad. "Thank you for teaching me about baptism and boomerangs. It's true, isn't it?"

"Yes, Amara. Families are forever. We can all return to our Heavenly Parents." Grandad hugged her.

"I love you, Grandad."

"I love you, too, Amara."

SHERRIE GAVIN was born and raised in upstate New York, USA. Always looking for romance and adventure, and with a love of writing, she traveled to Australia and fell in love with a true Aussie bloke named Bruce. 'Struth! They married and began adventuring together, joined by two beautiful daughters who are the loves of their lives. Sherrie has been lucky enough to have contributed to Linda Hoffman Kimball's Relief Society anthologies and *The Exponent II*. She also thinks that everyone should try throwing a boomerang at least once.

TATIANA LAWTON was born in Brisbane, Australia, but was raised up north on the sunny beaches of the Sunshine Coast. She was born with a love for life, art, and storytelling, and her pursuit to study for a degree in film and animation came as no surprise to family and friends. Moving back to Brisbane, Tatiana completed her four-year degree.

Since finishing her degree, she has been freelancing as an artist, contributing to short films as a concept artist, character designer, and storyboard artist. Tatiana has drawn her inspiration for this book from her Australian heritage and her appreciation for eternal families.